A Visit from St. Alphabet

POEM AND ILLUSTRATIONS
BY DAVE MORICE

COFFEE HOUSE PRESS

© 1980, 2005 by Dave Morice
LIBRARY OF CONGRESS CIP DATA
Morice, Dave, 1946–
A visit from St. Alphabet.
(1. Alphabet. 2. American poetry. 3. Narrative poetry.)
1. Alphabet rhymes. 2. Children's poetry, American. 1. Title
PS3563.087164V5 811'.54 80-24865
ISBN-13: 9781566891790 ISBN-10: 1-56689-179-5
1 3 5 7 9 8 6 4 2
PRINTED IN CANADA

A Toast
To U and I:
Merry X
And Happy New Y!

'Twas the night before X, when all through the Y
Not a letter was stirring, not even an I;
The S's were hung by the T's with care
In the hopes that St. Alphabet soon would be there;
The Z's were nestled all snug in their beds,
While visions of W's danced in their heads;
And U in your kerchief, and I in my cap,
Had just settled our words for a long writer's nap,—

When out on the paper there rose such a clatter,
I sprang from my sentence to see what was the matter.
Away to the period I flew like a flash,
Tore open the commas and threw up the dash.
The pen on the crest of the new-fallen O
Gave a lustre of adverbs to pronouns below;
When what to my wondering I's should freeze,
But a miniature A and eight tiny B's,

With a little word writer I never met—
I knew that it had to be St. Alphabet.
More rapid than pencils his pages they came,
And he wrote and typed, and called them by name:
"Now, P! now, O! now, E and T!
On, P! on, A! on, G and E!
To the top of the shelf, to the top of the wall!
Now tell away, yell away, spell away all!"

As dry leaves that before the wild W fly,
When they meet with a question-mark, mount to the sky,
So up to the bookshelf the pages they flew,
With the A full of nouns,—and St. Alphabet too.
And then in the books on the shelf I heard
The prancing and pawing of each little word.
As I drew in my ear, and was watching the sound,
Down the pages St. Alphabet came with a bound.

He was dressed all in A's from his B's to his C's,
And his D's were all tarnished with F's and G's;
A bundle of E's he had flung on his H,
And he looked like a poem just opening its page.
His I's, how they twinkled! his J's, how merry!
His K's were like roses, his L like a cherry;
His droll little M was drawn up like a bow,
And the N on his chin was as white as the O.

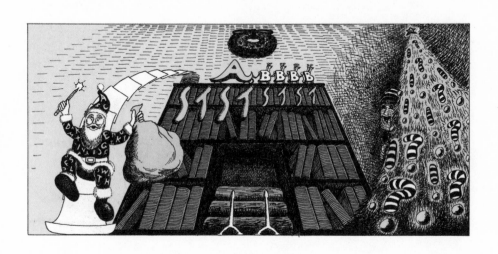

The ſtump of a P he held tight in his T,
And the Q it encircled his head like a V.
He had a broad R and a little curved S
That shook, when he laughed, in his anagrammed veſt.
He was U! He was W! He was X, Y, and Z!
And I laughed, when I saw him, alphabetically.
A wink of his I and a twiſt of his J
Soon gave me to know he had nothing to say.

He spoke not a word, but went straight to his work,

And filled all the pages; then turned with a jerk,

And laying his pencil aside of his nose,

And giving a nod, up the pages he rose.

He sprang to his A, to his B's gave a C,

And away they all flew like the down of a Z;

But I read in the sky, ere he wrote out of sight,

"Happy Alphabet to all, and to all a good write!"

COFFEE HOUSE PRESS is an independent nonprofit literary publisher. Our books are made possible through the generous support of grants and gifts from many foundations, corporate giving programs, individuals, and through state and federal support. This book received special project support from the Bush Foundation and the Woessner Freeman Family Foundation. Coffee House Press receives general operating support from the Minnesota State Arts Board, through an appropriation by the Minnesota State Legislature and from the National Endowment for the Arts, a federal agency. Coffee House also receives major funding from the McKnight Foundation, and from Target.

To you and our many readers across the country,
we send our thanks for your continuing support.